TWO SUNS OF MORCALI

TWO SUNS OF MORCALI

by Evelyn E. Smith

The idol was shaped like a handsome young man. The surface had a curious texture, as if skin rather than stone. There is a deceptive simplicity to this story about a rather forceful woman explorer (immensely practical, too) who goes to Grimalkin prepared for anything, including an attack on her life, but not for what does happen!

As the big interstellar liner nosed down to the airfield, a steady stream of reporters trickled out from the bar to meet her. The only notable on board, they knew, was Agatha Sherlip, the explorer, but she always made good copy. Though her veracity was sometimes open to question, her courage was not, and enough of the daring exploits on distant planets which she had recounted to the press, and subsequently expatiated upon in a series of best-selling volumes, had been substantiated to prove that a great deal of what she said was true.

And newspaper editors were always glad to have pictures of Miss Sherlip to brighten up their pages. As she posed at the head of the ramp leading down from the liner, the press marveled anew how, for one who was certainly no longer in her first youth, she managed to remain so wonderfully well preserved. Once one of the more sensational journals had hinted darkly of a mysterious fountain of youth far beyond Mizar, but the suggestion had been heavily pooh-poohed, for everyone knew that if Agatha had found any such thing, she would have immediately drained the fountain, bottled the water, and sold it to the public at a high price.

She made a charming picture, her long yellow hair blowing about her suntanned face, her brief skirts blowing about her long brown legs, as she called, "Mind those crates, Henry!" over her shoulder.

TWO SUNS OF MORCALI

"I am being most careful," replied a voice with a slight foreign accent, and a tall, handsome young man with a piece of sticking plaster on his forehead emerged, staggering—or, rather, surprisingly not staggering—under a prodigious number of packing cases. Porters rushed forward to help him, but Agatha waved them back. "Rare and fragile objects inside," she explained. "Henry knows how to handle them."

Henry grinned cheerfully. "Shall I take them to the car?" he asked, pointing to the pick-up truck.

"Please do, Henry, and then come back for the rest." Henry, followed across the field by the eyes of all of the female reporters, and some of the male as well, bore the boxes off with ease.

"Well, Miss Sherlip," the not-so-young man from the *Times* inquired, "was this trip as exciting as all the others? Or are the thrills of exploration beginning to wane at last?" He had vague hopes at which even he would have laughed, had they been put into words, that some day in the near future she might retire from the adventurous life and settle down, possibly with a deserving journalist who had, although she might not be aware of it, identified himself with her career from the very start.

Agatha smiled and tossed back her sun-bleached hair. "This was the most glorious trip I have ever had!" she cried.

All of them looked at her in astonishment. "More exciting than your journey down the man-eating rivers of Procyon V?" the *Standard* man asked.

She nodded happily.

"More exciting than your encounter with the savage saurians of Sirius VII?" queried the lady from the *News*.

"Oh, *yes!*"

"More exciting even than your disembodiment and subsequent reincarnation by the spirits of Fomalhaut IX?" the *Graphic* wanted to know.

"Far, far more exciting than all of them put together!" She flung her supple arms wide. "And far more thrilling. For on this voyage I discovered, beyond the stars, an intelligent life-form more interesting and unusual than any yet encountered in the Galaxy!"

The reporters pricked up their ears and turned their recorders to full power. She was continually running into new species, some of which had proven to be extremely interesting indeed. And intelligent life-forms were rare. "Tell us, Miss Sherlip, what were these creatures like?"

She smiled radiantly. "I shall tell you the whole story from the very beginning."

Seeing that this promised, like all of her narrations, to be a long one, the reporters sat down on the luggage of less lucky travelers who were forced to undergo the hoary ritual of customs (Agatha being exempt less because of her fame than because of the dangerous proclivities of her luggage, which frequently proved to be not only alive but ill-disposed) and listened attentively.

*

Well [she said] I won't bore you with the details of how I got to Regulus, because you can read about them in my *Edges of Nowhere*. No colonies out there, nothing but an outpost and a mine or two, so it doesn't pay for the stel-liners to include the system in their regular runs. However, I was lucky enough to catch hold of a freighter that was wending its way out to Regulus IV—Snellinger, you know—to pick up a cargo of ore. No passengers allowed, but a few credits in the right places got me a berth on her. Filthy dirty and there were a few of the usual contretemps because no one will, in spite of the lip service paid to female equality over the past few centuries, provide accommodations for ladies on any but the luxury liners. However, I am used to that sort of thing, and, if I do say so myself, handled the situation rather well. By the end of the trip, the crew regarded me either as a brother or as a terror.

The troops on Snellinger were delighted to see me again. I had been there before, some years back, to see whether the Regulus System were worth exploring, which it isn't.

Dreariest, most barren little agglomeration of planets you've ever seen. If it weren't for the rare minerals, I daresay the Federation wouldn't bother to keep an outpost there at all.

"Well, what brings you to our corner of the universe, Agatha?" the commandant asked heartily. "When you left, you said there was nothing of further interest in the Regulus System."

"There isn't," I told him, wishing to avoid a misunderstanding from the very start. "I'm interested in that new star I've been hearing about—Grimalkin, I think they call it—and this is the closest inhabited, in a manner of speaking, system to it."

The commandant paled and pulled at his mustache. "So those stories did get all the way back to Earth," he muttered. "Knew I should have stopped that fellow's mouth from the very start."

This was interesting because up until that moment I hadn't been sure but that I was on a wild mongoose chase. "Which fellow?" I asked, crossing my legs and lighting a cheroot.

"Just one of the miners telling tall stories. Didn't stop him. Thought it would entertain the men. Goodness knows, we have little enough to amuse 'em here. Aggie. . . ."

I slapped away his hand. "Let me speak to this miner," I demanded.

The commandant mopped his forehead. "He's dead."

"He is not either. Come on Freddie, cough up that miner. Remember—" I let my voice get soft, but not too tender "—the time you said you would do anything for me. This is your chance."

He sighed. "All right, Agatha, I'll have the man sent over." He spoke briefly into the communicator; then turned back to me. "Be a little time before he comes—the mine's on the other side of the planet."

I looked at him penetratingly. "Why do these stories of his bother you so much, Freddie?"

"Hate to see you haring off after nothing, Agatha. Hate to see you haring off. Agatha, dearest, won't you—?"

"No," I said. "What's this miner like? Where did he come from? How does he know about Grimalkin when our astronomers discovered it only a few years ago? Is he a reliable informant?"

"No, he isn't," the commandant replied eagerly. "Most unreliable. Makes things up. Spends all his time reading. Must've read every book in the library several times over. Probably that's where he got his story of a lost white race. . .

"So it's a *white* race, eh?" This seemed to upset him. "After all, why shouldn't they be white? There are blue aborigines in the Altair and Pollux systems, mauve on Capella, green on Arcturus and Procyon, orange on—"

"Spare me the catalogue, Freddie," I interrupted. "You know I've been everywhere and seen everything."

The commandant's face flushed mauver than a Capellan's. "Just wanted to point out that white is about the only original color left," he said huffily.

I blew a perfect heart in smoke. "Wonder whether he means white like us or a really dead white?"

"Does it matter?"

9

"No, I suppose you're right. Another intelligent life-form is interesting enough in itself without one's needing to puzzle over the subtleties of its coloration. Besides, I suppose I shall soon be seeing for myself, anyhow."

"Seeing for yourself?" He stared at me in horror. "You don't mean you're actually thinking of—?"

I blew another smoke heart "Why do you think I came to Regulus in the first place?"

A throat was cleared behind us, and, "You sent for me, sir?" a resonant tenor inquired.

It was the miner—I could tell from his clothes, and because a hasty washing had not succeeded in removing the professional grime. Otherwise he was a very presentable young man, tall, well-set up, and with an elegance and savoir faire that marked him as definitely a cut or two above the usual ore-digger.

"Yes," the commandant admitted, avoiding the man's eye, almost as if he were afraid of the fellow. "This lady would like to speak to you."

"If you don't mind," I put in, with the graciousness that has endeared me to natives throughout the Galaxy. The first thing one must do with informants is establish rapport.

His eyes looked me up and down and I knew I had established it. "At your service, madame," he murmured.

Although he spoke excellent Terrestrial, he was obviously not an Earthman. Human, of course; Terra had found, after sad experience, that it was wisest to bar all non-human intelligent life-forms from its outpost planets, except, of course, such aborigines as were inescapably indigenous. But I could not figure out from his accent which of the colonies he hailed from. Perhaps if I heard him speak some more. . . But obviously the commandant's presence was inhibiting him. It was inhibiting me, anyway.

"Well, Freddie," I said, "no doubt you have lots of odd jobs and so forth to do around the planet. Why don't you just buzz off, and I'll interview Mr. . . ?"

"Kruzmyt," the miner said, executing an impeccable bow as the commandant stalked off, muttering to himself. "Ilgu Kmzmyt. And whom have I the honor of addressing?"

I told him my name and offered him a cheroot, which he accepted and lit, after a quick glance at me to see what I was doing with mine. "Where are you from, Mr. Kruzmyt?" I asked casually.

"Here, there, everywhere," he answered, waving his arms expressively, if not explicitly. "I come, I go. I have been many places, seen many things."

"Where were you born?" I persisted.

"You might as well ask me who my father was," he shrugged. "The answer would be the same in both cases: I do not know. Is that why you have sent for me?" he asked, staring intently into my eyes. "To ask me of my origins?"

I could feel myself flush. "I understand that the legend of the mysterious white race in the Grimalkin system originated with you," I said abruptly.

His dark green eyes flashed. "It is not a legend. That star which you call Grimalkin actually consists of two suns, Bluuga, around which revolve eleven planets of assorted sizes, and Bnuuga, which revolves around the seventh of these, Morcali, a planet that corresponds to the description which I have read in your books of Paradise—only much better."

"In other words," I concluded, "an Earth-type planet."

He bowed. "Possibly. I have never been on Earth . . . although," he added courteously, "I have heard it well spoken of."

"How about this lost white race?" I asked.

"Lost white race, tcha !" He gave an impatient click of his tongue. "How these stories do get exaggerated in the telling."

"What do you mean?" Not that I had really believed the improbable tale, you know, but I must admit I was rather disappointed.

"They are not lost. They have always been where they are; it is their home—the planet of their origin. As a matter of fact, you are more lost than they. Look how many light years away you are from your planet."

But I was interested in their whereabouts, not mine. "Tell me about them. What are they like?"

He looked at me in astonishment. "Like you. Or me. Depending on sex, of course. What else could you expect from an Earth-type planet? Similar conditions produce similar results. Isn't that what your interesting science says?"

I regarded him thoughtfully.

"You think I'm lying, eh?" he said with heat. "Come with me to Morcali and see for yourself. The people may be hostile to strangers, but you can always shoot a few until they learn who is boss." There was a relish in the way he said boss that somehow led me to think he didn't mean me.

I crossed my legs. "Look, Mr. Kruzmyt, I'm an explorer, not an agitator. If trouble comes my way. I can handle it, but I don't go out of my way to stir it up. And the Federation frowns upon its citizens' going about waging private wars. I've already been warned about that."

"You could hardly call it war," he said eagerly, "or even trouble. Just a handful of ignorant natives; what could they matter?"

12

I raised my eyebrows. "Funny for you to call them that. Especially as you are one of them . . . or mean me to think so, anyway."

I watched his reaction narrowly, but he had himself well in hand and just smiled. "Why don't you check the truth of my story yourself? Come with me to Morcali." His voice grew soft. "It is spring on Morcali now. As a matter of fact, it is always spring on Morcali."

What was the fellow really after, I wondered. Rather too much trouble to have put himself to merely for the sake of my fair white body; besides, he could have had no idea who might respond to his carefully spread legends. Might just as easily have been Major Hathaway—fine chap and a splendid explorer, but hardly the alluring type. "Rather an expensive jaunt, you know," I temporized.

"You are worried about money? You need not be. I will help you to meet your ends. And mine. . . . Morcali is a very rich planet," he went on hastily. "All sorts of minerals, gems, natural resources abound there."

"I mustn't forget to take along my pick and shovel."

He frowned, and somehow 1 shivered, because he apparently expected people to shiver when he frowned. "No, I am serious. The people of Morcali, being simple savages, you know—unlike me, since I have acquired an education through diligent reading of the excellent though limited library available in the recreation center—worship the living god Morcal-Anri-Kruzmyt, who is enshrined in the capital city, Calin. Now this god has in his forehead—"

"Don't tell me, let me guess—a single eye, which is a perfect red ruby larger than a goose's egg."

He stared at me. "No, a star sapphire. But how did you know?" I pulled up my legs and rested my chin on my knees. "I've done some reading myself, you know."

He flushed. The color wasn't quite right—or was it my imagination? "So, you don't believe me, eh? Well, ask your commandant if I was not found on one of the Grimalkin planets by a spaceship that stopped there for repairs."

"How come they didn't report this paradise?" I asked, forcing myself to be skeptical.

"Briklus, Grimalkin XI, is not an Earth-type planet," he said, with obviously labored patience. "It is a barren piece of rock to which I had been exiled for political reasons which, I am sure, would not be of interest to you. I told the captain of the ship that I had been marooned there by another craft. He took me here because this was his destination. And it seemed they needed miners, so I stayed, although I am not," he smiled at the unnecessary statement, "a miner by profession. No one else but you knows I am other than I seem."

"Why are you telling me this, then?"

He grasped my wrist. The texture of his hand didn't feel quite right either, but I made allowances for the power of suggestion. "Because I see you are someone I can trust. Now you must trust me."

I didn't trust him, not one bit, but I was damned curious.

*

"Yes," the commandant said wearily, "it's quite true that he was found on Grimalkin XI by a ship that went off course and stopped there to patch up a meteor hole in its hull." He sighed. "He said the captain of the ship that had marooned him was his wicked uncle, which he seemed to feel was explanation enough. Only it turned out that the name of the ship supposed to have left him wasn't registered on any of the planets in the Federation."

I shrugged. "Well, there are lots of possible explanations for that. Pirates, for one thing—lot of them around and they're certainly not registered."

14

He looked at me coldly. "Oddly enough, that is just the explanation he offered us. Afterward. When he'd learned more Terrestrial and had been rooting about a bit in the library. I don't like this, Aggie—don't like it at all."

"Seems perfectly straightforward to me," I said, though, now that I'd had time to think things over, I realized it was a perfectly straightforward lie. I knew Kruzmyt's type—bit of an adventurer; you meet the kind all over the Galaxy. In fact some people have been unkind enough to apply the term to me.

"Well, there's one thing more. Didn't like to mention it, don't even like to think about it, but it rather sticks in my craw." I raised my eyebrows, questioningly. "The captain who picked Kruzmyt off Grimalkin XI made the routine report on planetary conditions, and there was one little factor that, well, bothered me."

"And that was?"

"It has no atmosphere." He tugged at his mustache. "And this Kruzmyt was living quite happily—well, not happily, I suppose, but he was living—without a spacesuit, without a shelter of any kind."

I got up. There was definitely more here than met the eye. "Freddie, I want to borrow your second-best scoutship. Looks to me as if this were a matter that could bear a little investigating."

The commandant was a little sticky about lending me the ship, but I reminded him of several tender episodes that had occurred the last time I was on Snellinger and in the end he gave in, as most men do when I really turn on all the voltage. However, I was curious about his attitude; it seemed more vehement than circumstances appeared to warrant. "Why are you so set on keeping me from Morcali?" I asked him.

"Well, if you must know, because I more than half believe Kruzmyt's story," he burst out. "And, you know, of all the intelligent life-forms that have been discovered on scores of planets, we have never turned up another example of the one we have found to be most dangerous of all."

"Don't be so damned theatrical," I told him. "You mean man, I suppose."

"I do mean man. Leave 'em alone, Aggie. Human beings who can breathe when there is no atmosphere, learn to speak a language fluently and adapt to a totally alien culture in a couple of months . . . who knows what other powers they might have? And, now that Kruzmyt has read the entire *Encyclopaedia Britannica* from cover to cover, who knows what dangerous knowledge he might be bringing to his people if you take him back?"

"Sorry, Freddie," I said, "but you're just making the prospect more and more alluring."

"Promise me this at least, Agatha," he insisted, catching hold of my wrist, "that you'll try not to antagonize them."

"Antagonize them!" I replied, indignantly wrenching myself free. "When have I ever antagonized natives?"

"How about those wars you started in Aldebaran and Castor?"

"They didn't start because I antagonized the natives; it was because the natives antagonized me!"

Freddie sighed and pulled his mustache. "You're a stubborn woman, Agatha," he said. "But promise me you'll be careful."

"I promised myself that a long time ago," I assured him.

I must say that Kruzmyt was a perfect gentleman through most of the two-month trip. And self-possessed. Didn't even turn a hair when I said casually, as I checked the gauges on the oxygen tanks, "I do hope Morcali has an atmosphere I can breathe. Because I'm rather partial to air, you know."

He grinned. "So they told you that story, did they? And you came, nonetheless. You're very brave, Agatha—I may call you Agatha?"

"Matter of fact, that was the very thing that determined me to come," I said quickly. "Proved, whatever else you were, you certainly weren't a terrestrial. But why is it that you don't need air? I thought you said Earth-type planets produced Earth-type people?"

"Oh, with variations," he shrugged. "Bound to be some differences, of course, since conditions can't be exactly the same. After all, Morcali has two suns; it revolves around one and the other revolves around it. Gives us a different psychology, you know." He gazed tenderly into my eyes. "I'm looking forward to seeing a Morcali sunrise with you. . . . Agatha."

Without meaning to, I nervously blew a heart-shaped smoke ring.

He looked at it. "Odd, how the very same shape can assume wholly different meanings in different cultures. For example, what you call a heart symbolizes the tenderest emotions to you, does it not?"

"Yes," I said. "And to you?"

He smiled. "To us it is merely a rather crude phallic symbol."

I hastily blew a free-form smoke ring. "Tell me—er—Ilgu," I asked, "how is it that with ail your—er—attributes, not breathing and so on, your people are not more advanced?"

He was silent for a moment, either choosing his words or making up a story. And he was breathing; I noticed that. Perhaps he was an optional breather. "It is because they are in the power of a corrupt priesthood," he said at last "Individual initiative is considered sacrilegious." And he heaved a sigh.

"That has something to do with your exile, hasn't it?" I asked shrewdly.

He nodded. "I had not planned to tell you this yet, Agatha, but I am the rightful ruler of Morcali. You may remain seated," he added graciously, although I had not stirred in my chair. "Because I sought knowledge, I was deprived of my title and my temporal powers and banished to a barren planet from which I was rescued by your fellow beings, to whom I shall always owe a debt of gratitude. Rest assured, Agatha, that when I am restored to the rank that is rightfully mine—"

"If you think I'm going to be on the restoration committee, or be the restoration committee itself, you're crazy," I said hotly. "I'm not going to be used as a cat's claw. Stealing that sapphire from the idol's forehead is what's supposed to turn the trick, isn't it?"

He smiled ruefully. "You are too clever for me, Agatha. True, the people—poor simple savages—believe that the power of the god rests in the sapphire. . ."

"Does it?"

"Agatha! You, an educated terrestrial to—to suggest a thing like that. But, of course, you are joking."

I gave him a weak smile. I had run into odoriferous set-ups before, but this one was stinking up all of Leo. "You can steal it yourself now that you're going to Morcali," I suggested.

He shook his head. "Impossible."

"It wouldn't look good for him if they caught the king, or whoever you really are, stealing the sapphire, would it?" I demanded. "But it's okay if an alien snaffles it because they can always burn her at the stake or eat her, or whatever you do." Although I was joking, of course, I watched his face, and he didn't look nearly horrified enough. I should have paid more attention to Freddie's warnings.

"My people are not that primitive," Ilgu said, in what I could not help but feel was too off-hand a manner. "Listen, Agatha, if you are caught stealing the sapphire, I can rescue you. But, if I am caught, you wouldn't know what to do." I must have still looked dubious, for he continued, "And the sapphire would be yours. It is as blue as your eyes, Agatha, and almost as beautiful."

I am, I must admit, partial to sapphires, but still I shook my head.

"How would you like to be Queen of Morcali, Agatha?" he asked softly. "As it happens, I do not have a wife."

I had been offered marriage by potentates before, mostly to shut my mouth. "Uh, uh," I told him.

Ilgu's tone changed from the melting to the brisk. "Well," he said, "how about a straight business proposition, then?"

"I'm listening," I said.

We had the terms all fixed up by the time we neared Morcali—so much in gems and precious metals, so much in art and artifacts. I knew I was sticking my neck out by trusting him at all, but, what the hell, a girl in my profession has to take risks. I'd done it before and made out all right.

We made planetfall on Morcali just at the double sunrise. First, pale green streaks appeared along the horizon, broadening to wide bands of jade and turquoise as the blue-green disk of Bluuga began to come into view. Then the jade was shot through with amethyst, deepening to purple and, with the emergence of the red-violet sphere of Bnuuga, the sky became a clear lavender, but a brilliantly vivid lavender, not the muted twilight mauve of Earth. A bird began to sing an odd trilling melody.

I never found out whether or not it really was spring all the time on Morcali, but it was spring when we came. Ilgu had told me where to land the ship, so we came to rest in a small valley hemmed in by low, round, pearl-toned hills. Trees more graceful than the terrestrial varieties thrust shapely branches laden with both blossoms—huge and scented—and jewel-like fruit up into the amethyst sky. Through grass of a greener hue than the grass on Earth, a purple stream rippled over translucent blue and violet crystals. The whole valley appeared to have been untouched by human—or humanoid—hands except for neat iridescent metal plaques affixed to the larger trees. Each was inscribed with the same legend in a script which, of course, I could not read. And there was air, wonderful, tangy, invigorating air. I breathed in vast lungfuls of it.

"We will have to wait for some time," Ilgu told me, as he courteously handed me out of the ship. "The god sleeps only when both suns have set."

"But how can an idol sleep?"

"I never said he was an idol!" Ilgu was reverting to primitivism. He knew what I was thinking be cause he followed his statement with a shamefaced laugh. "The . . . temple will be deserted then because, when the god sleeps—is supposed to sleep—the priests go to their quarters to sleep also," he explained. "No one to see you effect your entrance and exit."

"Oh," I said. "And in the meantime?"

"In the meantime we stay in this little valley. Is it not charming?" he added, with a proprietary interest based, I supposed, on the assumption that, as king, he felt the whole planet belonged to him. "All the fruit is edible. Help yourself." He plucked a bunch of transparent aquamarine berries from a bush and handed them to me with a courtly bow. I had met kings before, and I was suspicious. His manners were much too good for an authentic member of the royal fraternity.

"But won't some of the natives come across us?"

"They wouldn't dare!" He pointed to the signs. "Those declare this area to be—to be tabu. . . . Come, Agatha, let us relax, while we wait." He moved nearer to me.

"Relax one step closer, Ilgu," I warned him, "and you can steal your own sapphire."

He gave a strained laugh. "Well, you are king for the day, Agatha." And he sat down with his back against the wine-dark bole of a tree and stared into the distance. The light took on an increasingly greener tinge as Bnuuga began to sink in the south.

I'd better watch out for him after I'd completed my mission, I thought, as I sprawled on the grass at a safe distance from him and began to eat the fruit, which was, by the way, delicious. Lucky I'd got the terms of our contract in writing. It wouldn't stand in an Earth court, I knew, and maybe not even in a Morcali one, if they had such things, but it did give me a sort of hold over him, as it wasn't the sort of thing he was apt to want published.

I was a little sorry I'd agreed to do the job because it meant I could not go out and have a look at the country and its inhabitants. True, Ilgu had said the natives were hostile, but that didn't mean he had to be telling the truth. However, I had accepted the job and Agatha Sherlip's word was her bond.

"Ilgu!" I leaned toward him persuasively. "While we're waiting, why couldn't we take the scout and go visit some other city—on the other side of the planet? Perhaps the na—your people will be friendly after all. At any rate, they would not be able to communicate with Calin in time to warn the priests, would they?"

His face darkened. "My people are never friendly. Hostility toward strangers is part of our religious doctrine. And they would know about our arrival because there is a very complete communications system. Primitive, true, but nonetheless efficacious."

"But how is it worked?" I wanted to know. Then I heard the soft beating of the drums. "Oh, I see," I answered myself.

"You see!" He clutched my arm with his alien hand. "What do you see?"

"Figure of speech. I mean I hear—I hear the drums. That's what you mean, isn't it?"

He wiped his forehead. "You hear them too? . . . I—I thought. . .

"Aren't the drums what you meant?"

"Yes, yes. Of course. . . . The drums."

And, as they continued to beat, I suddenly thought of something. Now it was my turn to clutch his arm. "Ilgu, we wondered how you were able to breathe on Briklus. . .

He looked at me with wary eyes.

"But how did you get there in the first place? If your people are primitive, they don't have space travel. Or do they?"

His lips tightened. "No, they do not. I cannot answer your question now, Agatha. Not until after you have secured the sapphire.

And I couldn't get anything more out of him by way of explanation for the rest of the time we were in the valley. Bluuga began to set; it was growing almost dark. "Is it time now?" I asked Ilgu. He shook his head and pointed to where the rosy-purple rim of Bnuuga was peeking coyly over the hills. The drums continued to beat, louder and louder. I was beginning to get nervous, and so was Ilgu. "Your people send a lot of messages," I ventured.

He mopped the perspiration—aquamarine it was—from his face again. "I—I have never heard the drums before, that is, heard them beat so continuously before. . . . I must have underestimated . . . but so far as Regulus, how could that be?"

He was talking to himself more than to me. And suddenly all I wanted was to get out—away from this uncanny planet—and the hell with all the gold and jewels. "Let's go back!" I proposed.

"No, no, no!" His face was pale, a distinctly off-shade of pallor and it wasn't just the light either. "The people—the people are suspicious, but they do not know of our presence here. Or, if they do, they do not know what we' are after. . .

"Surely they would guess."

"No, because to them what we plan would be an unthinkable. You and I are sophisticates, Agatha," and his smile was almost a risus sardonicus. "You must try to understand them in the light of their own primitive psychology. They could not imagine such . . . utter blasphemy."

That, I felt, might be at least partly true: he wanted me to steal the stone for him, because, though he could free himself from superstition enough to conceive the idea of the theft, he could not bring himself to execute it. He pressed my hand. His was colder than I had ever felt human flesh before. "You'll be all right, Agatha, I assure you."

I wasn't so assured. But he kept between me and the ship and I didn't want to make a run for it and thus precipitate open hostilities between us.

By then I realized that he was perfectly capable of killing me if he saw I was going to be of no further use to him. Besides, I couldn't help thinking of what Freddie and the others back on Snellinger would say if I turned tail and ran back like that. And all because of a lot of silly drums; nothing more, really. They were growing louder.

The shadows lengthened in the south as Bnuuga set. I got to my feet. "Now?"

Ilgu shook his head again and pointed to a greenish glimmering in the east. "Bluuga will be up any minute. Better get some rest," he advised.

TWO SUNS OF MORCALI

I went to sleep in the grass, lulled by the rhythm of the drums. Ilgu remained underneath his tree, between me and the ship. I didn't know whether he was asleep or not.

Both suns were high in the heavens when I got up. Time apparently had little meaning here—for me, anyhow, although there appeared to be some discernable pattern for Ilgu in the movement of his suns. I washed in the purple stream and we ate a silent breakfast together.

Ilgu prepared it, for it was tacitly agreed that I was not to be trusted in the ship. After breakfast, he took one of my cheroots without waiting for me to offer it, and exhaled smoke that shimmered a pale purplish-olive in the alien atmosphere.

"I'd better brief you now," he said in a taut voice, as Bnuuga began to set and the light greened. "The instructions will be rather complicated, and you must obey them to the letter."

They were extremely complicated, and puzzling too. Bnuuga had risen again before I could figure out just what it was I was supposed to do. And even then I couldn't understand. Ilgu refused to explain. "Please believe me, Agatha. I know this planet and you do not. Should anything go wrong, I will not be able to save you unless you have followed my directions with the utmost precision."

"But it all sounds like a primitive ritual," I objected. "In fact, it sounds even more like something out of a fairy tale."

He didn't seem to understand quite what I meant; perhaps he was too nervous. "There is a very good reason for everything we do." He tried to smile. "You have trusted me so far, Agatha, why will you not trust me to the end?"

I had not trusted him; I did not trust him; I would not trust him. But there was nothing I could do, and so I agreed to carry out his elaborate plans, curious though they were.

And finally when Bnuuga began to drop slowly in the south, Bluuga also lowered in the west. "Come, it is time." Ilgu got up and threw away his cheroot. "Remember, always keep behind and don't speak to me or make any noise."

I nodded. He went off toward the east, turning to wave to me, as if I were staying behind. I waved back. When he had gone a hectometer or so, I rose and circled round to his left, being careful to keep out of his line of sight. From time to time he paused, to smell a flower or fasten his sandal, giving me a chance to catch up with him, but he never looked back to see if I were actually following. At the time it never occurred to me that I could simply turn back to the ship and desert him; I was already too much involved.

And so we proceeded on our strange journey toward the hills, he going on as if he were alone, never giving a sign that he was aware of my presence. I was reminded of Orpheus, but this Orpheus, so far as I could see, was more likely to be leading me into the underworld rather than out of it. A strange, sweet, and uncanny darkness began to drop down upon us. From the dusk the birds sang queer songs, and bushes and shrubs silhouetted into grotesque shapes. The drums were beating softly, insistently. I had been under an alien sun on many an alien planet, and none so nearly like Earth as this, and yet none so completely different. I was frightened, not for the first time in my life but for the first time in that way. None of my previous fears had had this peculiar aura of intangibility.

I stumbled and fell headlong into a bush. Its leaves caressed me, and the branches seemed to hold me gently, as if reluctant to let me go. Ilgu made no move to help. Only the fact that he slowed down a trifle showed his awareness of my plight. I realized that in some way I was not supposed to be there, but couldn't whoever—whatever it was, see me as well as him? Or was the perceptive sense on some level beyond or behind my comprehension?

I pulled myself away from the bush—regretfully, for it smelled so sweet—but I couldn't help making some noise. Ilgu's back stiffened, and then relaxed as I resumed my silent plodding along behind him. It was getting more difficult to follow him now that utter dark had fallen, the black, impenetrable night of a moonless planet, flecked with a star pattern that was all wrong for me. It was too quiet, and then I understood why. The drums had stopped.

For the first time in my life I began to wonder why I was where and who I was, why I had chosen the restless, roving life of the adventuress instead of being content to stay on my own planet, leading the healthy, normal, bovine life of a healthy, normal, bovine woman. What was I looking for? What was I trying to prove to myself? That I was better than anyone else? I knew that already.

At last we came to the crest of the hill and looked down upon Calin. And the people who had built that magnificent city of pale iridescent metals and soft dull stone in colors I had never seen before were certainly not primitives. Primitives could not have built that delicate filigree of bridges that interlaced the buildings, nor devised the crystalline pavements through which the purple waters could be seen flowing over their jeweled beds.

I looked at Ilgu's back. He clearly was not going to go any further. One by one the rose-violet lights of the city dimmed out as I watched from the hill. And then, finally, the blue lights of the huge pearly building that fitted Ilgu's description of the temple went out too. It was time. And from here on, the job was mine alone.

I descended, stumbling over the rough terrain, which grew smoother and smoother the closer I came to the outskirts of the city. The streets were deserted, as Ilgu had told me they would be. When the god slept, all slept. I thought it odd that a people as xenophobic as Ilgu had described his race to be should not at least have had guards posted about. Yet to guard them against whom? Strangers? There were no strangers, for this race was unknown to the rest of the Galaxy.

Lost . . . or perhaps it was the rest of us that were lost. There were many things Ilgu was going to have to explain to me, but the final explanation I would have to give to myself.

There was the temple looming ahead of me. I had not expected to reach it so soon. It almost seemed as if the crystal pavements had moved along with me, carrying me in the direction I desired. I paused uncertainly in the shadow of the huge edifice—so gracefully designed that it had not seemed nearly as large from the hilltop—afraid to enter. But I was equally fearful of facing Ilgu empty-handed. I realized it now; he meant to kill me once I had secured the jewel. Yet I was not sure, and, if the jewel meant so much to him, it would give me a bargaining power I did not have now.

A broad flight of stairs led up to the building in the manner traditional with temples the universe over. I mounted the steps one by one. Though they were shallow, my breath came short and harsh. I was growing a little old for this sort of thing, and I thought that, if this were not my last mission in the sense that I would not return from it, then it would be the last one I would ever undertake.

I took the sleep bomb Ilgu had given me and tossed it inside, where it exploded with a faint pop, releasing a luminescent cloud of soporific gas. I put on my gas mask and went inside.

The interior was vast, cavernous, dark, except for the faint glimmering of the gas, and silent. I longed to flash on my torch. Everyone should be asleep, but Ilgu had warned me not to show a light under any circumstances. I paused and, after a while, I could see a little. The dimly-viewed decor was lavish beyond anything I had ever seen, and somehow secular—more like the interior of a magnificent hotel lobby than a temple, but how could I presume to interpret an alien culture—and this was a very cultivated culture indeed—in my own terms?

The huge passageways that radiated out from the center of the lobby like the spokes of half a giant wheel were there, and the light which marked my ultimate destination glimmered faintly down one.

It grew larger and larger as I approached and finally resolved itself into a single turquoise flame flickering beside the recumbent figure of the god itself.

The idol had been shaped in the form of an extremely handsome young man, executed very much in the ancient classical style, and tinted in the lifelike colors with which the Greeks too had originally embellished their statues. So marvelously fashioned the image was that it actually seemed to be alive and sleeping. To my surprise, it had three eyes instead of one, and two of them were closed. Only the third, the enormous, truly magnificent star sapphire regarded me unwinkingly.

What a shame to take the stone and leave its even more precious setting! I tried to pick up the image—which wasn't *large* as such things go . . . actually very little more than life size. But it was nonetheless too heavy for me to lift more than a few feet from the floor. I let it drop—rather, I lowered it carefully, for I was reluctant to run the risk of damaging so beautiful a piece of workmanship. The surface, as I touched it, had a curiously resilient texture, as if it were skin rather than stone, and I reflected again on how advanced the people who created a work of art like that must be and what a pity it was I couldn't spend a day or two with them so that I could write a comprehensive volume about the planet. Still, the profits from my royalties have never equaled the resale value of my loot. That sapphire alone would bring more than three bestsellers would.

Taking a firm grip on myself, I wrenched the gem loose. And then I was aghast, fearing—in the surge of primitivism that welled up in me in those uncanny surroundings—that I had somehow injured the idol. But fortunately there was no socket underneath—that would have made the whole situation much uglier—just a bit of the skinlike covering came loose. The stone appeared only to have been glued on, which seemed very careless treatment of a jewel with such intrinsic as well as superstitious value. But again I was judging these people by my standards, not theirs.

Slipping the stone in my pocket, I turned and ran from that weird place as rapidly and as silently as I could. As I reached the end of the corridor, I could not help looking back over my shoulder and, for an instant, a trick of that flickering blue-green light made me think that the idol was leaning on one elbow staring after me. I closed my eyes and shook my head to clear my vision. When I looked back again, the figure was as it had been.

I made my way without mishap to the hilltop just as Bnuuga started to rise and pour its red-violet radiance over the nacreous rocks. Ilgu was waiting, his back toward me. We plodded back toward the valley, as we had come, not signifying awareness of each other's presence, not speaking. As we reached the ship, Bluuga, large and coldly green—like the eye of a greater god than the one I had just despoiled—emerged over the horizon. The drums started to beat again.

Ilgu shuddered. He stood still for a long moment; then slowly turned toward me, like a mechanical doll. "You have it?" he whispered hoarsely.

TWO SUNS OF MORCALI

I put my hand toward my pocket, but I did not take out the stone. "Yes," I said. "You want it, I suppose?"

"No, no, you keep it! The rest of the things I promised you are in the ship. For . . . heavens' sake, blast off before the suns get any higher." The sound of the drums was increasing in volume.

I looked inside the ship. The luggage compartment was crammed with crates of the wine-red wood. Apparently Ilgu had been even busier than I. I came to the door of the airlock. "You also promised me an explanation," I reminded him.

"I'll write you a letter," he said. "But, please, blast off now, before they discover what's happened."

"At least tell me what the drums mean!" I yelled, as he pushed me into the airlock.

"I don't know what they mean!" he shrieked, opening the inner door and thrusting me inside. "When I left Morcali, the drum had never been heard, or heard of, on the planet. Now, blast off, damn you!"

"I've got to take inventory first!" I cried.

"You can take it in space! If everything isn't according to the contract, sue me!"

Both doors clanged shut. This was one instance where discretion was the better part of squalor, so I blasted off. It was going to be rather a lonely trip without any company, even Ilgu's. Of course the ship could be put on automatic, so I wasn't bound to the control board, but it was a bit hard having no one to talk to, for I am not, as you know, the strong, silent type.

The first few days I amused my self by opening the crates and taking inventory of their contents. Everything Ilgu had promised me was there—jewels and ingots and art treasures. He had played absolutely fair with me. I had misjudged the poor fellow simply

30

because he was a liar, which the best of us can be at times, but now I knew his heart was in the right place—figuratively speaking, of course; for all I knew of his people's anatomy, he wore his heart in his heel.

A week passed and I began to grow a little tired of my expensive new toys, even of dreaming about the luxuries they would bring me upon my retirement, for I had definitely decided to retire now—while I was still young and able to enjoy my possessions. Seven more weeks before I would hit Snellinger. Even Freddie would look good by then. Was Freddie the man with whom I would choose to spend the rest of my days? Somehow he was not the ideal I had been subconsciously seeking.

I sat by the control board, although the ship was efficiently pursuing its own course by itself, and took out the sapphire to cheer me. It was the most beautiful jewel I had ever seen. Looking at the big blue stone, I could almost bring myself to believe that it did have powers above and beyond its financial one. And, with no one there to watch me, I could afford to be a little ridiculous. I rubbed the sapphire.

A hand reached over from the co-pilot's seat and took the stone from my limp fingers. "My eye, I believe," said a voice with a slight foreign accent.

I didn't dare turn to see who was sitting beside me in the copilot's seat. But I knew. I would have liked to faint just then, but I'm not the kind of woman who can do that sort of thing. I just sat there, rigid. "Did—did I do that?" I pushed the words through stiff lips. "Summon y-y-you?"

"By rubbing the stone, you mean?" the voice asked. Curiously enough, it seemed to be laughing. "Hardly. I've been here for some time. I just couldn't resist the temptation to startle you."

TWO SUNS OF MORCALI

I managed to turn my head toward him. It was he, the figure in the temple all right. What had I got myself mixed up in? He didn't seem to be angry, but that wasn't necessarily reassuring; it could be merely divine detachment with the ultimate penalty the same as that awarded by divine wrath.

"The stone itself has no particular value," he went on, "beyond the merely commercial one which is, of course, considerable. Of course the ignorant natives do think it has supernatural powers, which helps me to consolidate my rule, and which is why I wear it on my forehead in that rather ridiculous fashion."

"How did you get here?" I asked witlessly.

He laughed. "My dear girl, what a question to ask of a god!" I could feel myself paling. "You really fell for Ilgu's story hook, line, and sinker, didn't you?" he went on, in a more kindly tone. "Please notice my deft use of your idiom."

"It was a lie then—what Ilgu said to me!" I exclaimed, seizing desperately on any chance of passing the muck.

"Not really." The god smiled again. "He was merely trying to interpret our culture in terms of yours, and he isn't terribly bright, you know. . . . Nor is it," he added musingly, "an easy task."

"He must have thought the stone had mystic powers, otherwise why did he have me steal it?" I asked defensively.

The god laughed and tossed the sapphire in the air. "Well, I'm not saying he's completely free from superstition, but his real reason in having you steal the stone was to get me to follow you, so I'd be out of the picture for a while. In all of your people's books he read, the god—and I'm afraid he had a rather confused idea of what a god was; you mustn't confuse linguistic aptitude with real intelligence, you know—always follows the thief who steals the stone. Ilgu thought that if he could get me to go after you, he'd have another chance at the

32

kingdom. He's always trying to seize the kingdom; fellow has a one-track mind. My cousin, you know—from the feeble-minded branch of the line. He didn't think I'd have time to stop to teleport him back to Briklus before I joined you, because he underestimated my powers. By the way, in case you're interested, he's back on Briklus now, so busy teleporting air for himself from Morcali that he can't teleport himself back. Our usual treatment with criminals. Simple, but effective."

"He—he can teleport?" So that's how he'd got all the crates into the ship in such short order!

"Of course. Our whole family is talented; that's why we're the rulers. He can't do nearly as much as I can, of course. And he didn't think I could reach out beyond our system, let alone as far out as Regulus. Matter of fact, I had never thought of trying before. Probably—" he grinned at me "—with a little practice I could reach much farther than that."

I looked at him. My mouth was unbecomingly open.

"There are lots of questions you should be asking," he pointed out. "I have other powers too, especially useful in police work. I can share the sensory perception of any of my subjects, without his or its knowledge. I've been using Ilgu's eyes and ears—though not his taste buds; your food is really quite abominable if you don't mind my saying so—which is how I learned to speak the flawless Terrestrial on which you have not yet complimented me."

"It's quite remarkable," I managed to say.

"It was from reading your books through his eyes, that I got the idea of the drums," he said joyously, chucking the sapphire up in the air again. "Gave old Ilgu a turn, didn't they? I think I'll commute his sentence after a while; between us we've really given him a hard time. . . . He'd never have been able to seize the kingdom, of course,

TWO SUNS OF MORCALI

even if I hadn't stopped to dispose of him. Just now I'm the most popular ruler Morcali ever had; the king who gave the people the drum. And, frankly, I'm rather glad to be leaving the planet for a while. The drums were such a thumping success I can't get the people to leave off beating them. Got on my nerves too, after a while."

The sapphire described a glittering arc in the air and, missing the god's careless hands, disappeared through the grille leading to the air-conditioning unit. I gave a yip of dismay. "Don't let it trouble your pretty head, Agatha," the ex-idol said. "Plenty more where that came from."

"But, if that's so, why did you follow me?"

The god leaned over and gazed ardently into my eyes. His were bluer even than the sapphire.

"Can't you guess, Agatha?" he breathed.

As I have said, the ship was, fortunately, on automatic controls.

*

"Well," the man from the *Standard* said impatiently, "go on."

Agatha spread her arms wide. "But that's all. These crates which Henry is taking out to the truck contain the fee Ilgu paid me. I suppose the whole thing wasn't terribly ethical, but—" and she favored the press with an enchanting smile "—it all worked out all right in the end, didn't it?"

"But you haven't explained anything," the *Graphic* man protested. "For one thing, why did this Ilgu make you walk behind him all the way?"

"So the god wouldn't see her through his eyes, silly," the lady from the *News* snapped, "and know she was coming along. What I can't understand was how come none of the natives happened along in that valley."

Agatha smiled. "Oh, that's easily explained. I found out later; the people of Morcali have a very strong sense of private property. That valley was part of Ilgu's personal estate, and, just because he was a condemned criminal it didn't mean his property rights could be violated. The signs on the trees simply said *No Trespassing*. Even the king wasn't permitted to go there bodily without permission."

"And you really are going to retire?" the Graphic asked incredulously.

"Oh, yes—yes, that was my last trip. Anything else would be an anticlimax, don't you think?"

"If you ask me, I don't believe a word of it," the man from the *Times* said—tactlessly, of course, but he was no fool and he sensed the blight descending upon the passion he had cherished so long in secret.

Agatha was unperturbed. "That is your privilege."

"But what happened afterward?" the lady from the *News* asked eagerly. Then she blushed. "I mean after you and—er—the god reached Regulus. Only he wasn't really a god, of course?"

"Of course not," Agatha agreed.

"We were married when we reached Snellinger. Freddie was best man. Good sport, Freddie."

"Then. . . ?" With one accord the ladies and gentlemen of the press turned to look at the stalwart young man with the sticking plaster on his forehead, as he emerged from the airlock with another tremendous pile of crates.

"Henry, dear," Agatha said, "I think these ladies and gentlemen would like to speak to you."

"Delighted." Henry put down the boxes and smiled obligingly all round.

"I could hardly call him Morcal-Anri-Kruzmyt," she explained, "and since Anri is his given name, I call him Henry. Morcal is merely an honorific."

"But that's—that's miscegenation!" the *Times* exclaimed in horror, which was real enough even though the precise reason for it was not quite clear even to the reporter himself. "There are severe penalties for that!"

"Not that it's ever happened," the lady from the *News* murmured, with a frank smile at Henry, "because we've never before found a species worth miscegenating with."

"And even if your story isn't true—" the *Times* persisted.

"I thought you were positive it wasn't," Agatha smiled.

"—even if it isn't true and he's only a boy whom you picked up in the colonies—" here several of the pressmen clicked their tongues in disapproval "—he'd need a quota number. The government's very strict about that and it takes years. As if you didn't know. . .

"I think you'll find the Federation will think twice before it antagonizes so powerful a ruler as Henry," Agatha said with sweet shrillness. "It would be a little hard to apply the customary penalties to a teleport, wouldn't it? And don't forget that the people of Morcali still have Ilgu on Briklus, with the vast resources of the *Encyclopaedia Britannica* fixed firmly in his head. No, I think the Earth government would prefer to keep on friendly terms with a people that has such immense potentialities for peace and, of course, war."

"I don't believe he has any special powers at all," declared the heartbroken skeptic from the *Times*. "It's my belief he's just a non-quota immigrant you're trying to smuggle onto Terra."

"You think so?" Agatha raised her eyebrows. "Try to lift those then." She pointed to the pile of dark red wooden crates the divine Henry had set down.

The reporter strained, anxious to show at least that he was still in good condition despite the encroachments of the middle age that rendered him no competitor alongside the splendid youth, but he couldn't even lift a single box. However, and this helped salvage his pride, neither could the other reporters, nor even the field porters who came, anxious to display their skill in their own particular province, and who failed, bewildered and resentful.

"All right, Henry," Agatha said. "You can take the boxes to the car."

The young man smiled amiably at his audience, picked up the crates, and, balancing them all on one hand, bore the load off.

"It's a trick," the man from the *Times* said stubbornly. "That's all. Just a trick."

"Maybe," the lady from the *News* sighed, as she glanced after Henry's retreating form. "But, if so, it's a real cute one."

www.ingramcontent.com/pod-product-compliance
Lightning Source LLC
Chambersburg PA
CBHW020348130626
46549CB00003B/1347